THE MIXED-UP MUSEUM

By Gail Herman

Illustrated by Duendes del Sur

SCHOLASTIC INC.
New York Toronto London Auckland Sydney
Mexico City New Delhi Hong Kong

ISBN 0-439-20228-0

Copyright © 2001 by Hanna-Barbera.
SCOOBY-DOO and all related characters and elements
are trademarks of Hanna-Barbera.
CARTOON NETWORK and logo are trademarks
of Cartoon Network © 2001.
All rights reserved. Published by Scholastic Inc.
SCHOLASTIC, HELLO READER, and associated logos are trademarks and/or registered trademarks of Scholastic Inc.

20 19 18 17 16 15 14 13   5 6 7 8 9/0

Designed by Maria Stasavage

Printed in the U.S.A.
First Scholastic printing, May 2001

The Mystery Machine squealed to a stop. Velma jumped out. "We are late!" she cried. "The Museum of Natural History will close before we get to see the dinosaurs."

3

"Scoob and I are sorry, Velma," Shaggy said. "But like, we *had* to stop for pizza."

"Don't worry, Velma," Daphne said. "There is time to sec the new show."

Fred looked at a map. "The Great Dinosaur Hall is this way!"

"But the cafeteria is the other way!" said Shaggy.

Velma led the gang through the jungle room. Shaggy read a sign. "Gorillas in the Wild."

"Ratch out!" Scooby shouted. A gorilla was swinging right at them!

"Don't worry," said Velma. "These gorillas are puppets. They are wired to move and make noise so we can see how they live in a real jungle."

Shaggy sighed. "Like, I wish those bananas were real."

Next they came to the elephants. The animals raised their trunks. "Rakes?" asked Scooby. "Fakes!" said Velma.

"Even those peanuts!" said Shaggy.

Finally, they reached the Dinosaur Hall. Large dinosaur skeletons peered down at them. A crowd of people oohed and ahhed.

GREAT DINOSAUR HALL

9

"Look at that!" Velma said. "A rea
brachiosaur skeleton!"

"Amazing!" said Fred.

"Jeepers!" said Daphne.

"Rikes!" said Scooby.

10

The brachiosaur looked too real. Its great jaws opened and closed. "I am starving," Shaggy said.

"Re roo," said Scooby, licking his lips.

Shaggy turned to a security guard. "Like, where's the best place to chow down?" he asked.

"The cafeteria is this way," the guard said. He waved his arm, and hit a sign.

"Oops!" said the guard. "I have new glasses. And I still can't see very well. But I can take you to the cafeteria. I have to go that way to start closing the museum."

A few minutes later, Shaggy and Scooby had
emptied the salad bar, the soda machines, and
everything in between.

All at once, the cafeteria lights flickered.
On, off.
On, off.
Shouts echoed all around. Something was happening!

"Come on, Scoob!" shouted Shaggy. "We have to find the others!"

They raced back to the Dinosaur Hall. The brachiosaur skeleton swung its mighty head. It snapped its jaws. One leg moved, then another. "It is alive!" a boy shouted.

Everyone ran in fright. "Don't panic!" Velma
called.

A shadow fell over the gang. The dinosaur roared, right over their heads. "Run!" Fred said.

They raced past the elephants. The elephants raised their trunks and stomped their feet. They sounded angry.

Scooby and the gang sped past the gorillas.
The gorillas were swinging from vine to vine.

"Jinkies!" cried Velma. "What is going on here?"

"It looks like we have a mystery to solve," said Fred.

"But we can't hang around," said Shaggy. "It is closing time."

"Ret's ro!" Scooby agreed.

"Hmm," said Daphne. "Would you stay for a Scooby Snack?"

Awhooo! Howling filled the hall.

"Rikes!" cried Scooby, "a ronster." He jumped into Shaggy's arms.

"How about *two* Scooby Snacks?" asked Velma.

"Rokay!"

"Great," said Velma.

"Now, let's split up and look for clues," said Fred. "Daphne, Velma, and I will find the security guard. He might know something."

Scooby and Shaggy headed down a long, dark hall. With every footstep, they heard strange animal sounds. Then they heard a low, loud moan coming from behind a door. A sign on the door read KEEP OUT!

KEEP
MUSE
WORK
ONL

"Zoinks! It is a scary jungle beast!"
Shaggy yelped.

"Ruh-roh!" Scooby barked. They raced back
the other way. They crashed right into Velma,
Fred, and Daphne.

Shaggy said, "There's a monster behind that
door! The sign says KEEP OUT! And, like,
that's what I want to do!"

27

"I have an idea," Velma said.

She flung open the door. Then she flipped on the light.

"Thank goodness!" said a voice.

"Hey, it's the security guard," said Shaggy.

"What are you doing here?"

The guard waved around the room. The gang saw buttons and levers and switches. "This is the museum control room," he explained.

"I thought so," said Velma. "I bet you stepped inside to close down the museum. But you could not see very well."

"I turned off the lights by accident," said the guard. "And when I tried to find the switch, I pressed all the wrong buttons."

"And everything went crazy!" Velma finished.
With some help from the gang, the guard
quickly fixed everything. The museum grew
quiet.

Then came a long, loud rumbling sound.
Everyone jumped. "That's just Scooby's
tummy!" said Shaggy. "Hey, can you flip one
switch back on? The one for the cafeteria?"
"Scooby Dooby Doo!" barked Scooby.